This book belongs to

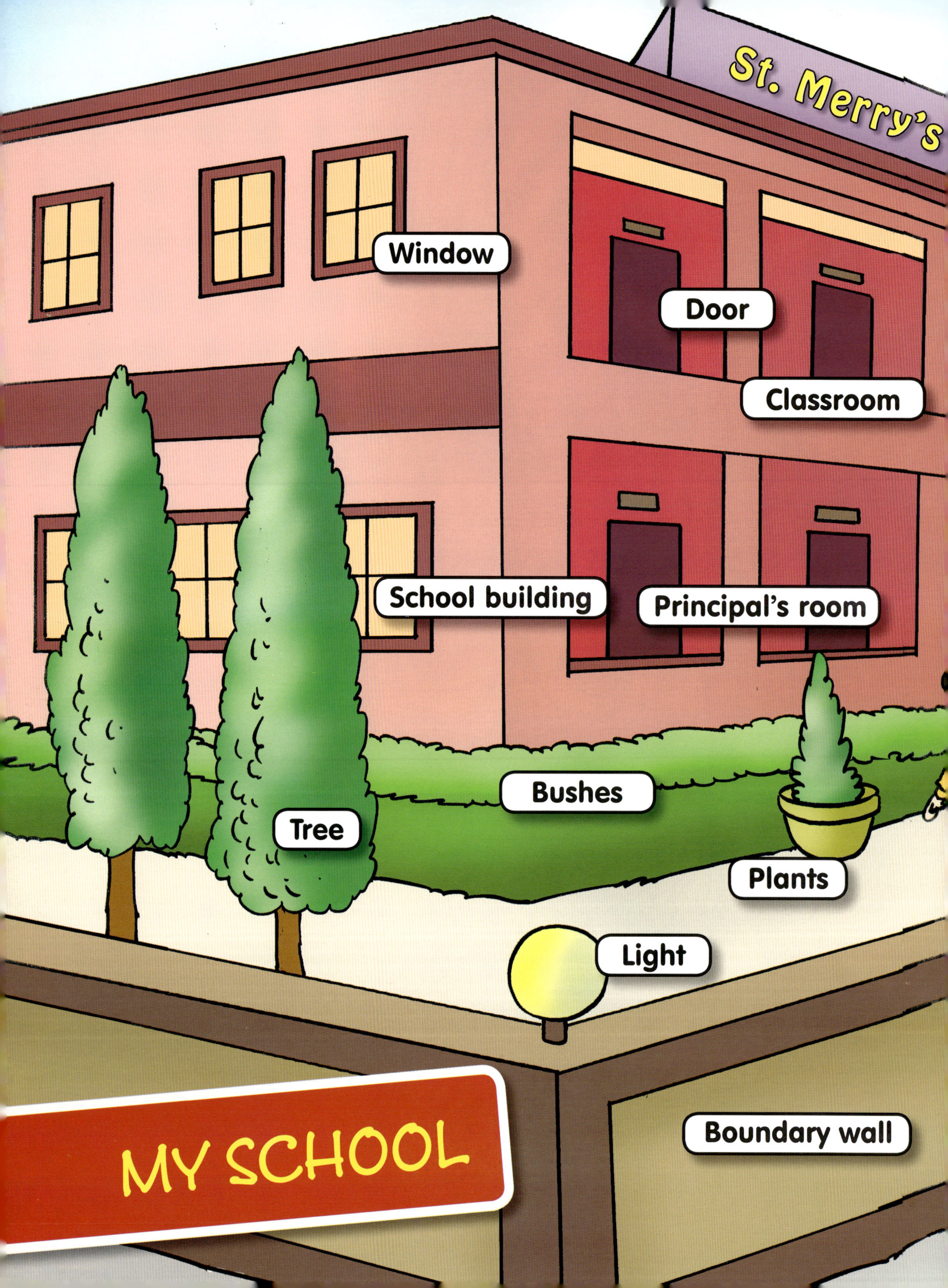
St. Merry's
Window
Door
Classroom
School building
Principal's room
Bushes
Tree
Plants
Light
MY SCHOOL
Boundary wall

School
Clouds
Activity room
School bus
SCHOOL BUS
Stairs
Teacher
School bag
Gate
Pavement
Student

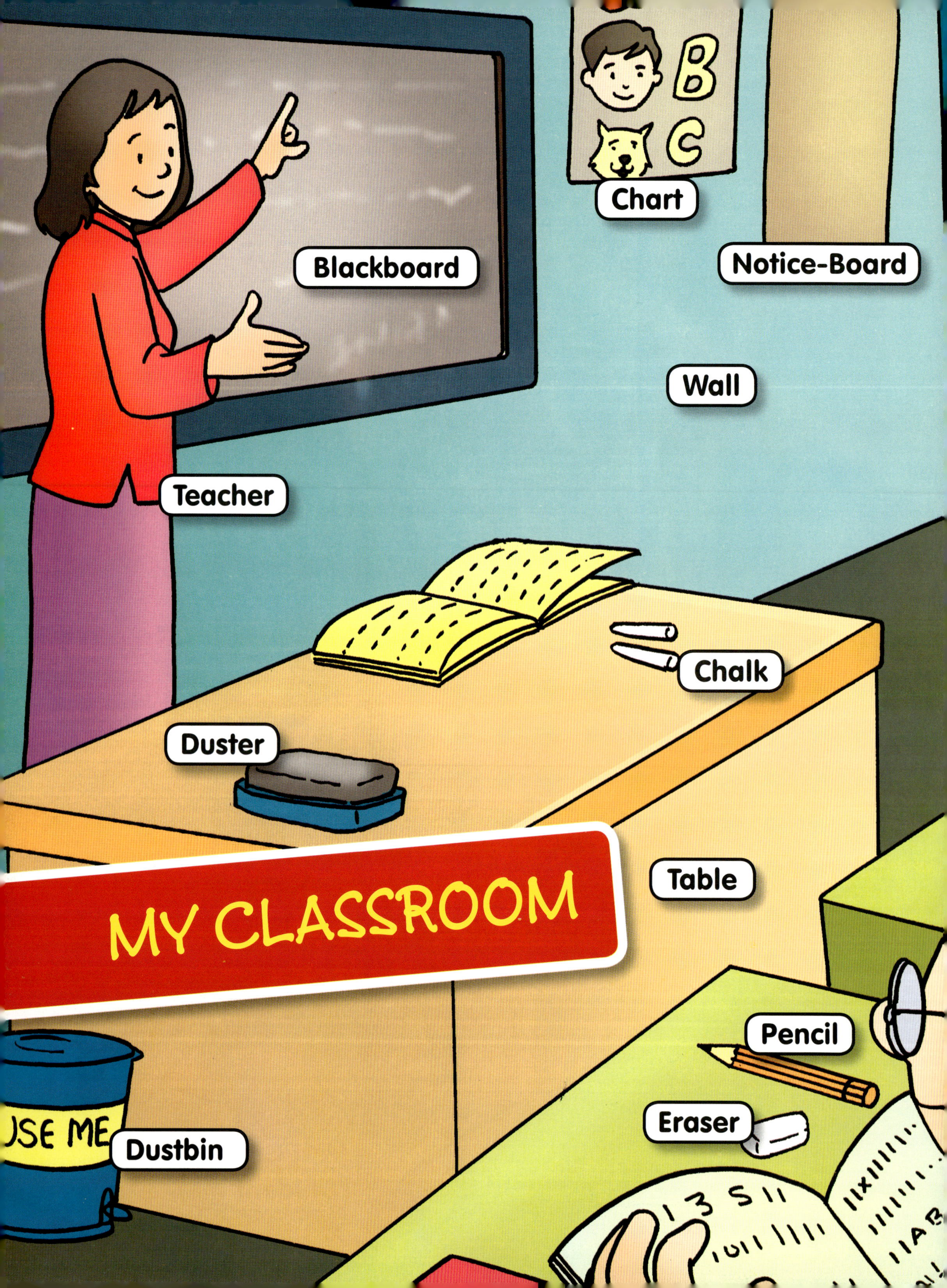

Chart
Blackboard
Notice-Board
Wall
Teacher
Chalk
Duster
Table
MY CLASSROOM
Pencil
Eraser
Dustbin

Window
Poster
Door
Books
Student
Pen
Desk
Bench

PRINCIPAL'S ROOM
Map
Filing cabinet
Monitor
Keyboard
Mouse
Files
Principal
Parent
Cellular phone
Pen stand
Globe
Mr. N.P.Gaur
Telephone
Nameplate
Table

Wall clock
Trophy
Books
Door
Student
Chair
Carpet

Gardener
School Building
Plants
Slide
Watering Pipe
Shuttlecock
Girl
Racket
Grass
Seesaw
Boy
Flower

Ball
Tree
Bush
USE ME
Dustbin
Swing
PLAYGROUND

AUDITORIUM
Balcony
Exit sign
EXIT
Microphone
Audience
Seat
Chief guest
Stage light
Speaker

KIT
Exit gate
Photographer
Camera
Curtain
Spotlight
Actor
Stage

Painting
ACTIVITY ROOM
Water Mug
Colour Tube
Teacher
Table
Activity Table
Chair
Dustbin
Floor
Scissors
Glue

Guitar
Violin
Pencils
Crayons
Drawing
Cube
Student

SILENCE PLEASE
Wall
Bookshelf
Books
Librarian
Table
Student
Pen
Table

Door
Bookrack
Assistant librarian
Ladder
Chair
LIBRARY ROOM

SCHOOL MAP

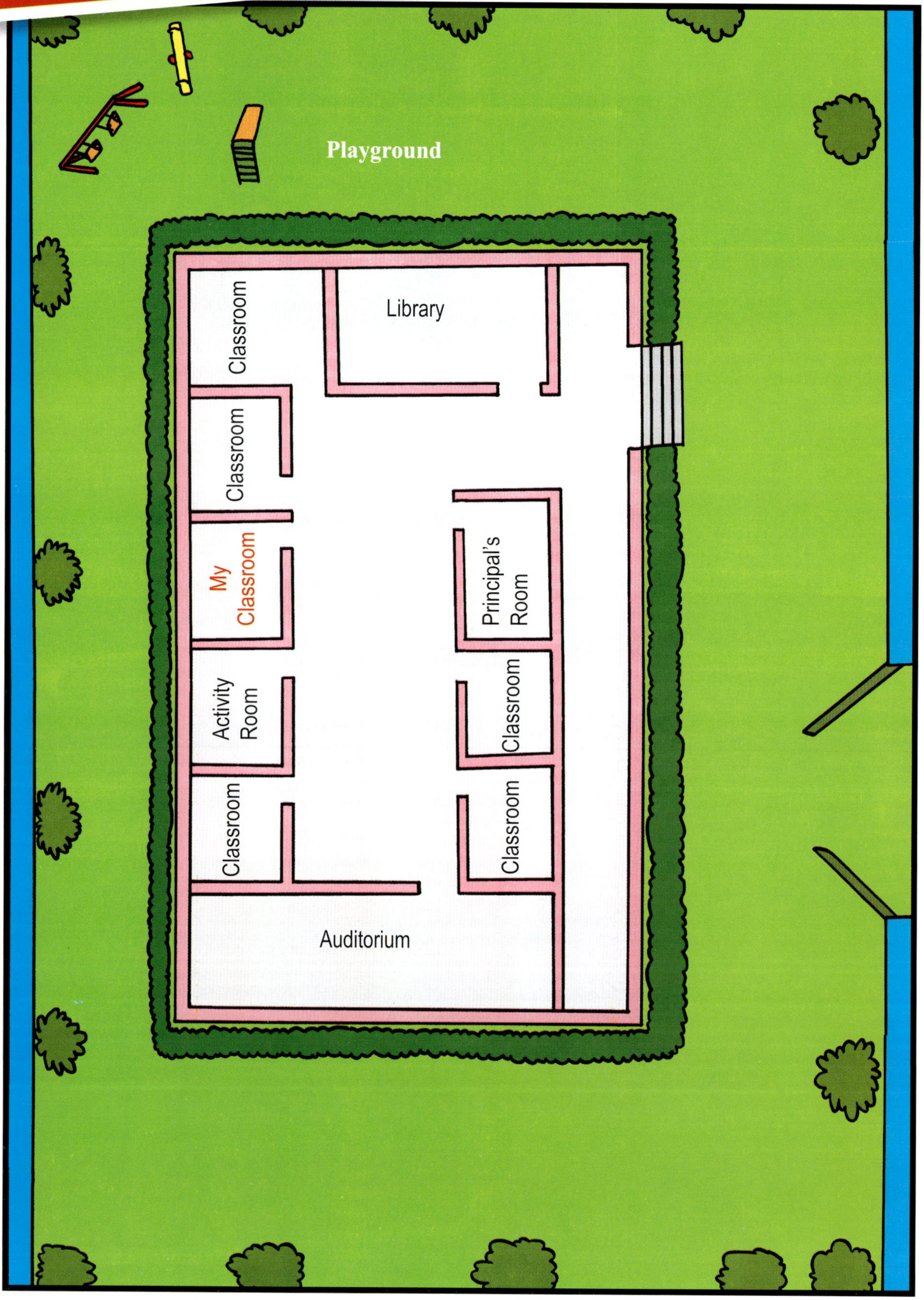
Playground
Library
Classroom
Classroom
My Classroom
Activity Room
Classroom
Principal's Room
Classroom
Classroom
Auditorium

Guitar
Violin
Pencils
Crayons
Drawing
Cube
Student

SILENCE PLEASE
Wall
Bookshelf
Books
Librarian
Table
Student
Pen
A B C
Table

Door
Bookrack
Assistant librarian
Ladder
LIBRARY ROOM
Chair

SCHOOL MAP

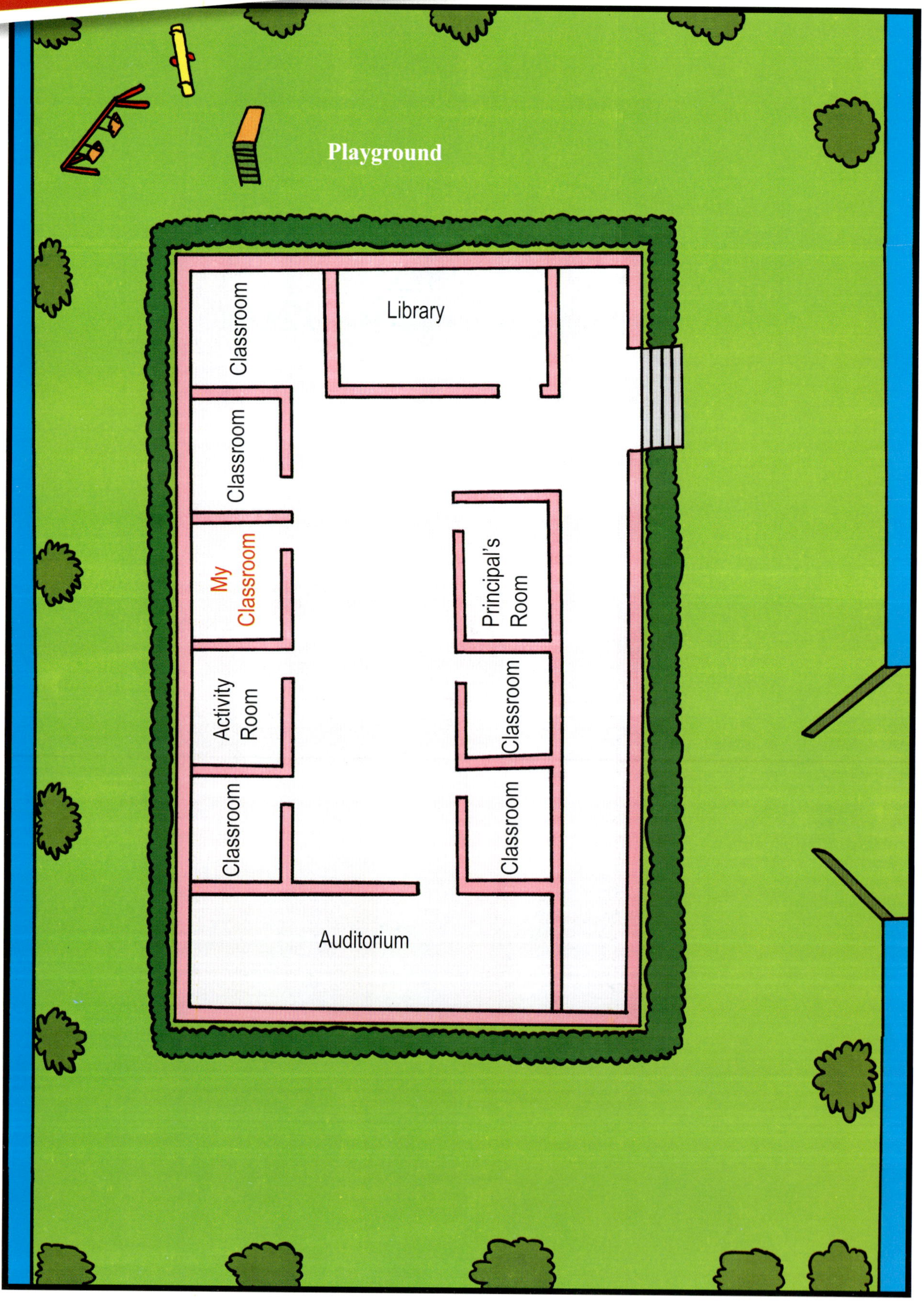
Playground
Library
Classroom
Classroom
My Classroom
Activity Room
Classroom
Principal's Room
Classroom
Classroom
Auditorium